It was an ordinary day in the Pickles' house. Everyone was busy. Tommy and his friend Chuckie were having a play date.

"This game is too easy," Tommy sighed. He tossed the big, round ball a few feet away to Chuckie.

"Aw, come on, Tommy, it's fun," said Chuckie.

Tommy's mom, Didi, was on the phone. Grandpa was watching TV with the volume turned all the way up. Angelica, Tommy's cousin, was playing in the kitchen.

"Turn your hearing aid up, Pop," said Didi.

Tommy's dad, Stu, was in his workshop putting the finishing touches on a new invention.

"What's that?" asked Stu's brother, Drew.

"It's the fabulous WonderWinder," said Stu. "Now let's give it to Tommy for a test run. . . ."

Tommy was still trying to get Chuckie to play a different game.

"I gotta idea," said Tommy. "How about if we stand on our heads?"

"That might give me a headache," Chuckie said.

Chuckie watched as Tommy struggled to stay on his head.
After a while his face turned bright red. He felt dizzy.

"Are you okay?" Chuckie asked.

Bonk! Tommy slammed down on the floor. "Wow! I can
see stars! Are you sure you don't want to try?" he asked.

"Okay, forget about that," said Tommy. "I gotta 'nother idea. Vroom, vrooom! Let's play with my little town and my cars."

Tommy showed Chuckie a little red fire truck. "Wanna use this? The bell rings when you roll it on the ground."

"Thanks, Tommy," said Chuckie. "But this nice dump truck is okay. Fire trucks get in trouble. I don't want any trouble."

Tommy rolled the fire truck. It rolled past the toy box and stopped in front of—trouble!

"Tommy, what's that, that, that . . . THING . . . over there?" said Chuckie. He pointed to the strange toy.

"I dunno," said Tommy.

"Where did it come from?" asked Chuckie.

"I dunno that either," said Tommy. He crawled toward the strange toy and reached for it.

"Don't touch it!" shouted Chuckie.

"Aw, Chuckie," said Tommy. "It's just a toy. See?" Tommy picked up the WonderWinder. It was heavy.

"Be careful," said Chuckie. He took a few steps back and clutched his blanket while Tommy wound the key in the back of the toy.

Tommy set the toy back on the ground and watched to see what it would do. Nothing happened.

"Oh, well," said Tommy. He turned away. Then, suddenly . . .

Ping! There was a loud noise. The beady little eyes on the toy began to flash and twinkle. "Grrrrrrawk!" screeched the toy.

"Ahhhhh!" Tommy screamed.

"It's gonna get us!" shrieked Chuckie.

The WonderWinder lurched toward them. Angelica ran out from the kitchen to see what was going on. "Hey, what are you babies doing?" she shouted as she stepped into the playpen.

"Angelica, watch out!" cried Chuckie.

"Oh, please," said Angelica. "You don't expect me to fall for that old trick. What is it, a monster?" Angelica started to laugh. "Ha, ha, ha! You babies are so stupid."

"Grawk!" screamed the WonderWinder. Angelica turned around as the WonderWinder went for her.

"Ack!" Angelica shrieked. "Get away from me!" She swung at the monster with her doll.

"Run, Angelica, run," cried Tommy and Chuckie.

"Grawk, grawk, grawk," went the toy. It had Angelica's Cynthia doll in its clutches.

"Wah!" cried Angelica. "I want my Cynthia!"

The WonderWinder squeezed the doll in its arms and began marching forward. It crushed the tiny village. It stepped on cars. It twirled its antennae. It screeched. It buzzed.

"Come on, guys, we gotta do something," said Tommy. "We gotta stop that thing and save Cynthia!"

"But what can we do?" asked Chuckie.

"I gotta idea!" said Tommy. "Maybe we can't stop that thing, but I know somebody who can. . . ."

Bravely, Tommy crawled past the wild windup toy. He dug deep into the toy box to find what he needed.

"Reptar to the rescue!" Tommy shouted.

He ran toward the awful monster, holding Reptar out in front of him. "Rah!" yelled Tommy.

"Grawk!" screamed the WonderWinder. Reptar pushed the WonderWinder and it fell over. Suddenly it was silent.

"Gimme my dolly," said Angelica. "I'm getting out of here." She scowled at Tommy and went back to the kitchen.

Chuckie helped Tommy clean up the mess the WonderWinder had made. Then they sat in a circle to play a nice quiet game of ball. "Phew!" said Tommy.

Stu peeked into the living room. He saw the WonderWinder standing near the toy box where he had left it.

"Gee, I don't think they even noticed it," said Stu. "I guess I need to give the WonderWinder more pizzazz. Maybe a supercharger would do the trick. . . ."